Zen Ben

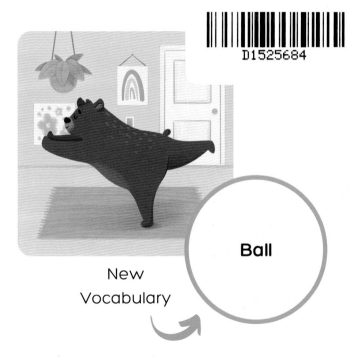

New
Vocabulary

Ball

Just Right Reader Inc.

Ben is not zen yet.

1

Ben will get zen.

He goes into his den.

Ben gets his legs set.

Ben goes up.

Ben puts a leg on the mat.

Ben puts his back on the ball.

Ben tips his leg back and up.

Ben is zen.

Ed, Jen, Ken, and Ted are not zen!

It is OK.

Ben hugs his cubs.

He tells the cubs, "Hop on my back for fun!"

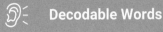 Target Phonics Skill

Short /ĕ/ CVC Words

CVC Fun

- Tap out the sounds in each word to help your reader sound out the word.

- Tap your shoulder for the first sound.

- Tap your elbow for the vowel sound.

- Tap your wrist for the final consonant sound.

- Then, put them all together faster!

Decodable Words

Ben	Jen	Ted
den	Ken	tell
Ed	leg	yet
get	set	zen

High-Frequency Words

and	goes
are	he
for	into

Decodable Words can be sounded out based on the letter-sound relationships.

High-Frequency Words are the most commonly used words. Your reader will begin to recognize them.

CVC Words are consonant-vowel-consonant words, like cap or big. The vowel sound is always short.